MARMALADE

BEANS

my
family
is
scrummy

ORCHARD BOOKS
338 Euston Road, London NW1 3BH

Orchard Books Australia
Level 17/207 Kent Street, Sydney, NSW 2000

First published in 2010 by Orchard Books

ISBN 978 1 40830 936 0

Text and illustrations © Leigh Hodgkinson 2010

The right of Leigh Hodgkinson to be identified as the author and illustrator of this work has been asserted by her in accordance with the Copyrights, Designs and Patents Act, 1988.

A CIP catalogue record for this book is available from the British Library.

1 2 3 4 5 6 7 8 9 10
Printed in China

Orchard Books is a division of
Hachette Children's Books,
an Hachette UK company.

www.hachette.co.uk

For fun activities and to find out more about Leigh Hodgkinson, visit:
www.wonkybutton.com

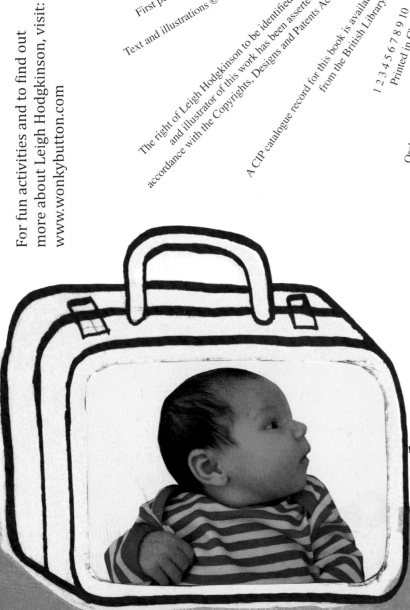

FOR tiny B, AN especially SCRUMMY ingredient

& a HUGE HOORAH to the ORIGINAL sandwich FAN (THE EARL)

ScRUmmY!

Leigh Hodgkinson

ORCHARD BOOKS

My dad says that every family has its own special magic recipe with lots of

SCRUMMY

stuff inside.

And I have just decided that my family is kind of like a

sandwich.

A sandwich can be a bit too BORING and everyday, but it ALL depends on what's inside, you see.

So, this is what is inside MY family sandwich . . .

<u>INGREDIENT NUMBER ①</u>

I am the **CHEESE** in MY sandwich
(the most <u>IMPORTANT</u> ingredient in my opinion).

This is because I am stretchy and **BENDY** and everything.

Also, my favourite colour is DEFINITELY yellowy-orangish.

You see, yellowy-orangish is nice and SUNNY - just like ME!

BOING

BOING

INGREDIENT NUMBER ②

The twins are the frilly green salady stuff that tickles and ALWAYS seems to be there (even if sometimes you don't want it to be).

INGREDIENT NUMBER ③

OH! I nearly forgot the mayonnaise. Adding a little dollopy splurge of this makes sandwiches **much** tastier, you know.

SPLISH SPLOSH SPLAT

Mayo

Mayonnaise is SO smooth and creamy - just like our dog Mr Honeycomb!

HOWEVER,
it is also slightly gooey, and too much makes everything go ALL SOggy. (Which is exactly what happens to Mr Honeycomb after a refreshing puddle dip.)

INGREDIENT NUMBER ④

A sandwich can't be a proper sandwich without the slices of **breAd** that hold everything together.

EVERY

family has a person or two who kind of does the same thing.

❶ CHeese

❷ green stuff

❸ MAYo

❹ BREAD

In MY particular case
it's my mum and dad.

Like nice fresh bread, they are

soft and **spongy**

which is good for hugs
and napping on.

So, now that the
sandwich is ready,
I proudly present my
fabulously

filling,

family

super-

SANDWICH . . .

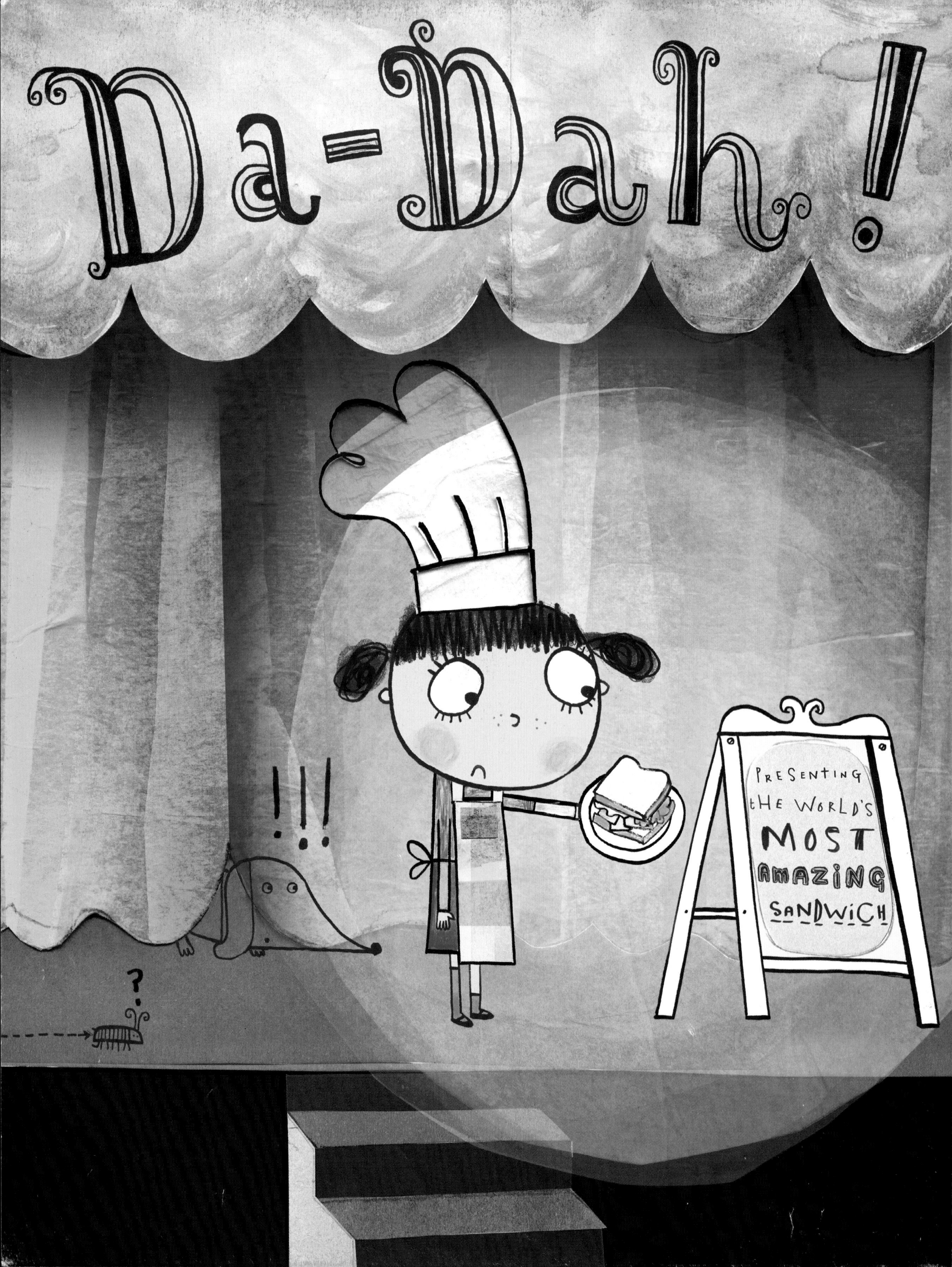
Da-Dah!
!!!
?
PRESENTING
tHE WORLD'S
MOST
AMAZING
SANDWICH

Oh deAR,

my sandwich isn't quite as **AMAZING** as I had hoped.

But **WAIT!**

There's **oodles** more room inside.

I'm sure I could **squish** and **squeeze** some more bits and bobs in there to make it a bit more exciting and unusual.

Now, let me see . . .

how about . . .

...BANANAS!

I think bananas would be good in MY sandwich.

I happen to LOVE
ice cream AND penguins.

I think there would
D E F I N I T E L Y be enough
room in our fridge for a penguin to stay.

I am putting a GIGANTIC chunk of chocolate in my sandwich, too.

It is **milk** chocolate, you see.

And you know who likes to *slurp*

milk, don't you?

KiTTeNS!

Oh, I have **ALWAYS** wanted a kitten. They are so sweet and purry.

Now, for the finishing touch to my sandwich . . .

...some **marshmallows!** They are very light and fluffy, just like sheep (which is good news as they won't squash everything too much).

Oh dear!
This sandwich is getting a bit too tall and "teetery" now.

I hope it doesn't fall over and make a BIG . . .

MESS!

OOPS!

I'd better clean up the hORRIBLE splodgy splat and make everything ALL shiny and new before anybody sees it.

Thinking about it, perhaps those last few ingredients were a bad, __BAD__ idea . . . Thinking about it, perhaps my family sandwich was perfect as it was . . .

... as monkeys would be cheekier and NOISIER than the TWINS.

And the penguin would be a bit

<u>too</u> interested in poor old

<u>GLITTERGILLS.</u>

MR HONEYCOMB

probably wouldn't think that a kitten is <u>QUITE</u> as sweet as I do.

tHe DOG +Kitten HOUSE

And MUM AND DAD

would most likely prefer a **SheePLeSS** garden.

MUNCH

CRUNCH

(BAAA-D SheePS!)

LUNCH

PHEW... just in time!

LucKILY, Mum is impressed with the sparkly kitchen floor and asks if I want a **treat** for being a *goody-goody*-two-shoes.

I say, 'YES PLEASE'

BUT

as long
as it isn't
anything with
bananas or
ice cream or
chocolate or
marshmallows in it.

I say the thing that I would
REALLY love,
the thing that would be the
nicest treat in the
whole world, is . . .

...a good old **cheesy** salad sandwich.

Mmmmm...

SCRUMMY!